Nursery Rhymes

Itsy Bitsy Spider

and Other Best-loved Rhymes

alphabet soup

an imprint of

WINDMILL BOOKS

New York

Published in 2009 by Windmill Books, LLC
303 Park Avenue South, Suite # 1280, New York, NY 10010-3657

Illustrations by Ulkutay & Co. Ltd.
Editor: Rebecca Gerlings
Compiler: Paige Weber

Publisher Cataloging Data

Itsy bitsy spider and other best-loved rhymes / edited by Rebecca Gerlings.
p.   cm. – (Nursery rhymes)
Contents: Itsy bitsy spider—Little Jack Horner—The queen of hearts—
Jack be nimble—Little Boy Blue—Peter, Peter, pumpkin eater—
Ring around the rosie—Ladybug, ladybug—Peter Piper—Mary, Mary quite contrary.
ISBN 978-1-60754-128-8 (library binding)
ISBN 978-1-60754-129-5 (paperback)
ISBN 978-1-60754-130-1 (6-pack)
1. Nursery rhymes   2. Children's poetry   [1. Nursery rhymes]
I. Gerlings, Rebecca   II. Mother Goose   III. Series
                398.8—dc22

Printed in the United States

CONTENTS

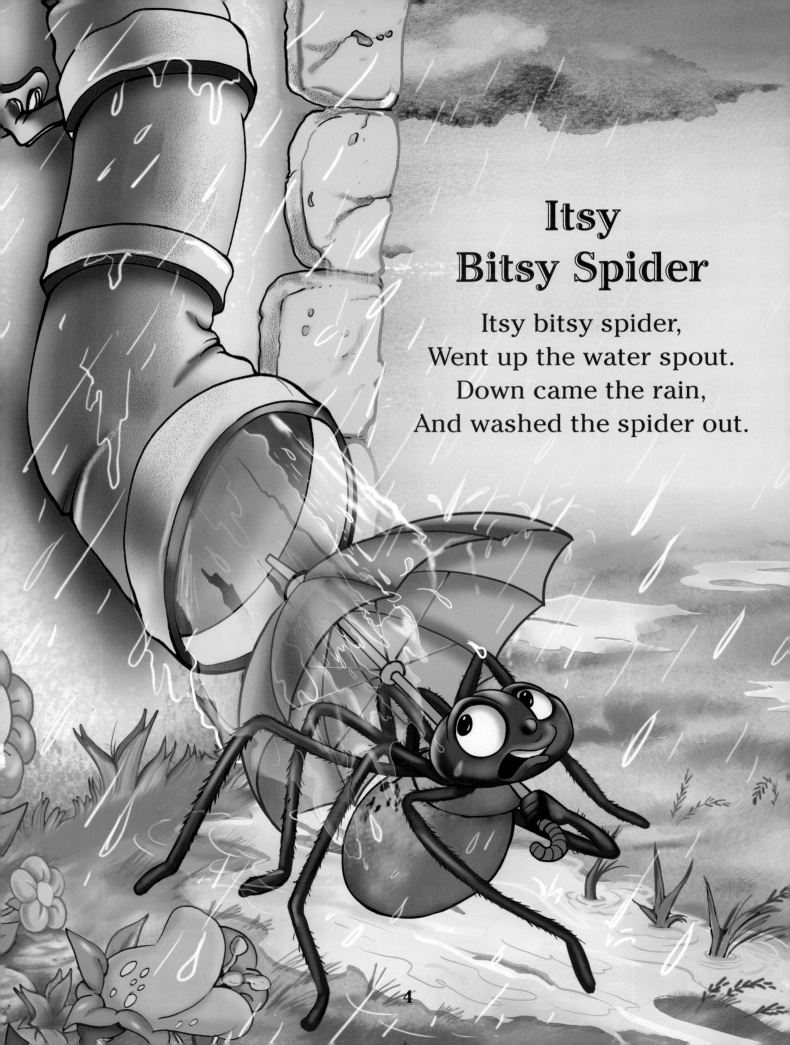

Itsy Bitsy Spider

Itsy bitsy spider,
Went up the water spout.
Down came the rain,
And washed the spider out.

4

Out came the sun and
Dried up all the rain.
And itsy bitsy spider
Went up the spout again.

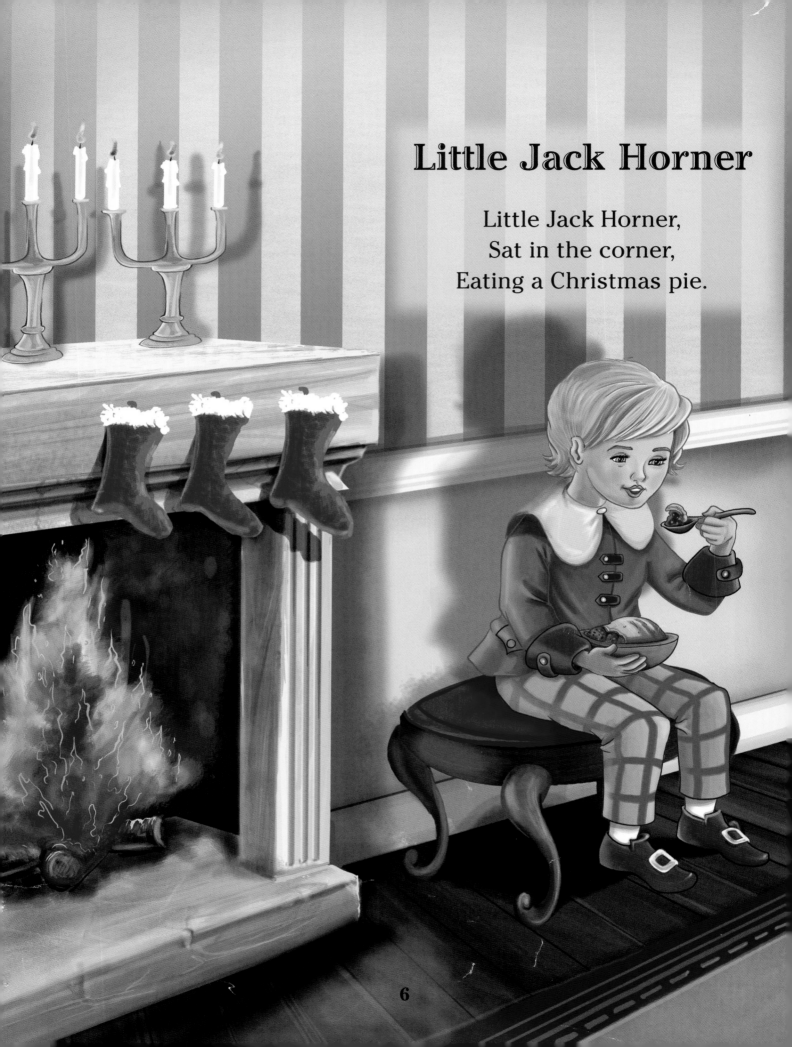

Little Jack Horner

Little Jack Horner,
Sat in the corner,
Eating a Christmas pie.

He stuck in his thumb,
And pulled out a plum,
And said, "What a good boy am I!"

The Queen of Hearts

The Queen of Hearts,
She made some tarts,
All on a summer's day.
The Knave of Hearts,
He stole the tarts
And took them clean away.

The King of Hearts
Called for the tarts
And beat the Knave full sore.
The Knave of Hearts
Brought back the tarts
And vowed he'd steal no more.

9

Jack Be Nimble

Jack, be nimble,
Jack, be quick,
Jack, jump over the candlestick.

Little Boy Blue

Little Boy Blue,
Come blow your horn.
The sheep's in the meadow,
The cow's in the corn.

11

Where is the boy
Who looks after the sheep?
"He's under the haystack,
Fast asleep."

Will you wake him?
"No, not I,
For if I do,
He'll be sure to cry."

13

Peter, Peter, Pumpkin Eater

Peter, Peter, pumpkin eater,
Had a wife but couldn't keep her.
He put her in a pumpkin shell,
And there he kept her very well.

Peter, Peter, pumpkin eater,
Had another but didn't love her.
Peter learned to read and spell,
And then he loved her very well.

Ring Around the Rosie

Ring around the rosie,
A pocket full of posies,
Ashes, ashes,
We all fall down.

The King has sent his daughter,
To fetch a pail of water,
Ashes, ashes,
We all fall down.

17

The birds upon the steeple,
Sit high above the people,
Ashes, ashes,
We all fall down.

The wedding bells are ringing,
The boys and girls are singing,
Ashes, ashes,
We all fall down.

Ladybug, Ladybug

Ladybug, ladybug, fly away home!
Your house is on fire, your children are gone.
All but one, and her name is Anne,
And she crept under the pudding pan.

Ladybug, ladybug, fly away home!
The field mouse is gone to her nest,
The daisies have shut up their sleepy red eyes,
And the bees and the birds are at rest.

21

Ladybug, ladybug, fly away home!
The glowworm is lighting her lamp,
The dew's falling fast, and your fine speckled wings
Will flag with the close-clinging damp.

22

Ladybug, ladybug, fly away home!
The fairy bells tinkle afar.
Make haste or they'll catch you and harness you fast
With a cobweb to Oberon's car.

23

Peter Piper

Peter Piper picked a peck of pickled peppers.
A peck of pickled peppers Peter Piper picked.

If Peter Piper picked a peck of pickled peppers,
Where's the peck of pickled peppers Peter Piper picked?

Mary, Mary, Quite Contrary

Mary, Mary, quite contrary,
How does your garden grow?
With silver bells and cockleshells,
And pretty maids all in a row.

26

ABOUT THE RHYMES

For hundreds of years, children have been reciting and memorizing nursery rhymes. Many of us can still recite these unusual poems, but few stop to ask where they come from. It may come as a surprise that nursery rhymes are more than just pleasant children's verses. In fact, they often reflect historical events from the period in which they were written.

Some nursery rhymes contain hidden political messages. They might mock a prominent leader, party, or other group. But why would an author conceal a political message in a child's poem? Probably because at the time, a more direct challenge to the establishment could have been punishable by death! As a result, nursery rhymes create a lasting connection between the present and the past.

Many of these rhymes were passed down orally, so many different interpretations of their meanings exist. The following are the most popular or commonly accepted interpretations of some of the rhymes. If you are curious about the other rhymes, don't stop here! Each rhyme has a special story to tell.

Jack Be Nimble

Most people agree that the origin of this rhyme comes from Black Jack, an English pirate who was notorious for escaping from the authorities in the late sixteenth century. However, the rhyme may refer to the old tradition of "candle leaping" as practiced at some English fairs. This tradition goes back to an old sport of jumping over fires. In the lace-making schools of Wendover, Buckinghamshire, it was traditional to dance around the lace-makers' great candlestick, and it is thought that this also led to the practice of jumping over a candlestick.

Little Boy Blue

There is a belief that the little boy in this rhyme may be a reference to Cardinal Thomas Wolsey, an Englishman who lived during the Tudor times. The Cardinal was a wealthy, rude character who turned many people against him. The phrase "come blow your horn" points to Wolsey's arrogance. He had much to boast about, including the fact that he graduated from Oxford University at age fifteen, earning the nickname "Boy Bachelor."

Ring Around the Rosie

This rhyme has its origin in English history during the Great Plague of London in 1665, or perhaps during the first outbreak of the plague in the 1300s. Plague symptoms included rosy, ring-shaped marks on the skin – hence "Ring Around the Rosie." Pockets and pouches were filled with sweet-smelling herbs, or "posies," that people carried in the belief that the disease was spread by bad smells. It is thought that "ashes, ashes" refers to the burning of dead bodies. In another version, "Ring-a-Ring-o' Rosie," the phrase "ashes, ashes" changes to "a-tishoo, a-tishoo," as sneezing was another plague symptom.

Mary, Mary, Quite Contrary

The Mary in this English rhyme is supposedly Mary Tudor, or Bloody Mary, who was the daughter of King Henry VIII of England. Queen Mary was a strict Catholic and the garden referred to in the rhyme is an allusion to graveyards, which were increasing in size as Protestants were killed for maintaining the faith that Mary was so opposed to. *Silver bells and cockleshells* were common words that referred to instruments of torture. *Maids* refers to a device called The Maiden, which was used to behead people. This was the original guillotine!

Ladybug, Ladybug

A ladybug is an insect with a red body and black spots, also known as a ladybird. If a ladybug landed on a child, the child would sing "Ladybug, Ladybug," adding "fly away home," if the insect did not fly away. Ladybugs were held in high esteem by land owners because they ate other creatures that posed a threat to their crops. As a sign of respect and thanks, farmers would sing the "Ladybug, Ladybug" rhyme before burning their fields to kill unwanted pests.